MW00807557

To my friends and family
for your love and encouragement.
Through my journies of adventures,
you are always home in my heart.

Serineh, our very own illustrator,
for your brilliance and hard work!
You made this vision so special and complete.
Thank you for this wonderful experience
and your boundless support.
—K.O.

Deoji's
Traveling
Bandana Band

Kelly O'Connor

Serineh Eliasian

Preface

Words you need to know so the story will flow.

Deoji is pronounced the way you spell dog, D.O.G.

Now you can spell "dog"
and say his name perfectly!
Deoji is a curious dog
with a wondrous sense of adventure.
He loves music and making friends
everywhere he goes.
Join Deoji as he is introduced to new animals,
countries and music from all around the world.

Glossary:

Didjeridu, also spelled **Didgeridoo**
pronounced [dij-uh-ree-doo, dij-uh-ree-doo].
The Didjeridu is
an Australian wind instrument.

Zerbaghali Drum,
pronounced [Zer-buh-gali].
The zerbaghali is
a goblet-shaped hand drum that
is played in the folk music of
Afghanistan.

On a spring afternoon, under the
sun's bright golden glow,
Deoji wakes from a nap in a comfy
pet shop window.

He is a small and rather cute puppy.
Black nose, brown eyes,
and fur so soft and fluffy.

Deoji spends most of his day
making music in the pet shop.
He plays his squeaky toy as an instrument
while singing, doo wop, bebop and maestro
take it from the top!

He always wonders
what it would be like
to explore the outside.
He dreams of listening to music
in a taxi and going for a ride.

Deoji sees the door
was left open wide.

With hopes of adventure
he dashes outside.

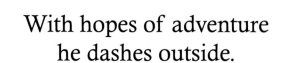

New York City is a very busy,
and fun place to see!
He hears music and wonders,
"where could that be?"

The music brings him to Central Park.
He's so excited, he let out
the happiest BARK!

Deoji looks amazed
and cannot believe his own eyes!
Are those animals playing in a band?
What an awesome surprise!

They have a snow leopard
playing a zerbaghali drum.
His paws make the beat,
ba rum bum bum bum!

There's also a koala
playing the didgeridoo.
It sounds like an owl,
hooot hooot hooo!

Plus a well dressed,
singing penguin pair;
who harmonize with
a Polar Bear!

The band is finished playing
and soon it will be dark.
Deoji starts to walk and realizes
he's lost in Central Park.

He really wishes
he had brought a snack.
He finds a carousel to rest
and thinks how to get back.

The park is now dark,
and Deoji feels a little scared.
Now he wishes he were better prepared.
He never told anyone he was going to leave.
He wonders, "what have I done?
This I cannot believe!"

He starts thinking about
the pet shop crew.
They were so nice,
giving him treats he loved
to chew.

When the temperature is cold,
they turn on warm heat.
Now he is stuck sleeping
in a carousel
on cold concrete.

He finally falls asleep
and night passes into a sunny day.
He wakes to hear music
and the sound is not too far away.

He finds a girl playing guitar
and decides to stay.
He can watch for a while
and maybe learn to play.

She takes a break
and offers to share her lunch.
He likes the veggies
that have a crispy crunch!

She says, "I'm Nelly and this is Goldie, my favorite guitar. It is small, which allows me to carry it far."

Nelly notices he's the puppy that went missing from a pet shop yesterday. She quickly calls the pet shop to say, "We are on our way!"

His dreams come true in the taxi
when they hear the music play.
Nelly says she lives in a big theater
with room for him to stay.

Nelly asks Deoji,
"Do you want to join a band
that does a worldwide tour?"
His ears perk up, his tail starts to wag,
as he imagines the fun adventures
that are in store!

She says, "The Bandana Band and I performed in Central Park yesterday." He barks in excitement, this was his wish when he saw that same band play!

This is truly a dream come true!
This is exactly what he
envisioned he'd do.

Nelly tells him,
"Now Deoji, never wander off
without telling someone, please."
Deoji snuggles next to Nelly
with assuring ease.

Deoji promises never to leave
without letting someone know
where he will go.
Deoji's cannot wait to meet the band and
practice for his first show!

Illustrations and book design by Serineh Eliasian.
The illustrations for this book were done digitally.
Typeset in Calisto MT
and the display type was hand-lettered.

ISBN 978-1-7353280-0-3 (ebook)
ISBN 978-1-7353280-1-0 (paperback)

For more information visit www.travelingbandanaband.com